Fluttering Butterflies

Mary Elizabeth Salzmann

Consulting Editor, Diane Craig, M.A./Reading Specialist

A Division of ABDO
ABDO
Publishing Company

visit us at www.abdopublishing.com

Published by ABDO Publishing Company, a division of ABDO, P.O. Box 398166, Minneapolis, Minnesota 55439. Copyright © 2012 by Abdo Consulting Group, Inc. International copyrights reserved in all countries. No part of this book may be reproduced in any form without written permission from the publisher. SandCastle™ is a trademark and logo of ABDO Publishing Company.

Printed in the United States of America, North Mankato, Minnesota
102011
012012

 PRINTED ON RECYCLED PAPER

Editor: Katherine Hengel
Content Developer: Nancy Tuminelly
Cover and Interior Design and Production: Kelly Doudna, Mighty Media, Inc.
Photo Credit: Shutterstock

Library of Congress Cataloging-in-Publication Data

Salzmann, Mary Elizabeth, 1968-
 Fluttering butterflies / Mary Elizabeth Salzmann.
   p. cm. -- (Bug books)
 ISBN 978-1-61783-191-1
 1. Butterflies--Juvenile literature. I. Title.
 QL544.2.S25 2012
 595.78'9--dc23
                      2011023249

SandCastle™ Level: Transitional

SandCastle™ books are created by a team of professional educators, reading specialists, and content developers around five essential components—phonemic awareness, phonics, vocabulary, text comprehension, and fluency—to assist young readers as they develop reading skills and strategies and increase their general knowledge. All books are written, reviewed, and leveled for guided reading, early reading intervention, and Accelerated Reader® programs for use in shared, guided, and independent reading and writing activities to support a balanced approach to literacy instruction. The SandCastle™ series has four levels that correspond to early literacy development. The levels are provided to help teachers and parents select appropriate books for young readers.

Emerging Readers
(no flags)

Beginning Readers
(1 flag)

Transitional Readers
(2 flags)

Fluent Readers
(3 flags)

Contents

Fluttering Butterflies 4
Find the Butterfly 22
Glossary 24

Fluttering Butterflies

There are many kinds of butterflies. They live almost everywhere in the world.

Butterflies have long bodies. Their bodies are covered with tiny hairs.

Butterflies have two large, round eyes. They can see very well.

Butterflies have two **antennae**. Each one has a small bump on the end.

Butterflies have four wings.
They fly during the day.

Butterfly wings have tiny **scales**. The scales can be many different colors.

Butterflies have six legs. They can taste things with their legs!

Butterflies have long **tongues**. They drink **nectar** from flowers.

Butterflies **spread** their wings in the sun. This helps them stay warm.

Find the Butterfly

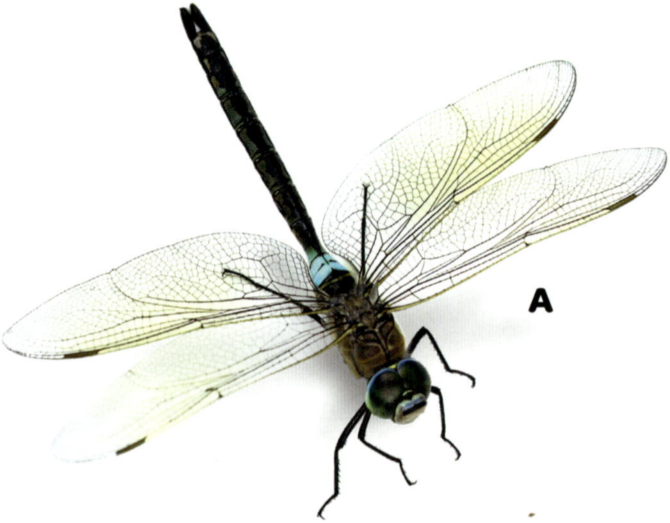

A

B

C

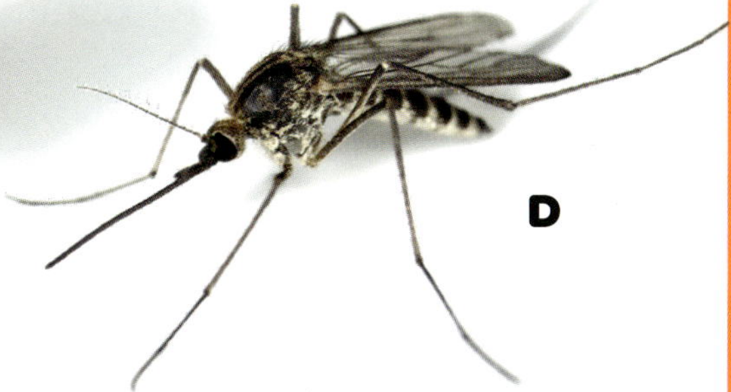

D

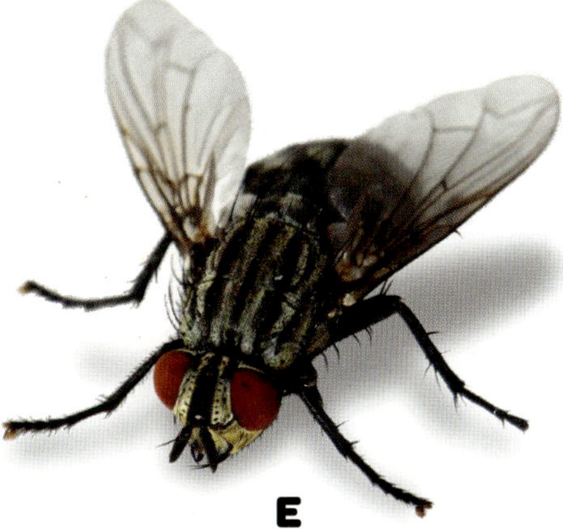

E

F

Answer: C

23

Glossary

antenna – a feeler on an insect's head.

scale – one of the small, thin, plates that cover the wings of butterflies and moths.

nectar – a sweet liquid found in flowers.

spread – to stretch out or unfold.

tongue – the movable muscle in the mouth that is used for tasting and swallowing.

Edison Twp. Public Library
340 Plainfield Ave.
Edison N.J. 08817